THIS BOOK BELONGS TO

Coll and His White Pig

Holt, Rinehart and Winston
New York / Chicago / San Francisco

Coll and His White Pig

by Lloyd Alexander

Illustrated by Evaline Ness

Holt Owlet Books is a paperback picture book series, carefully chosen for merit and popularity from a distinguished backlist of children's literature.

Owlet Titles You May Enjoy:

ALL IN THE MORNING EARLY by Sorche Nic Leodhas; illustrated by Evaline Ness
ALPHABET OF GIRLS by Leland Jacobs; illustrated by John E. Johnson
THE BEE-MAN OF ORN by Frank R. Stockton; illustrated by Maurice Sendak
A CERTAIN SMALL SHEPHERD by Rebecca Caudill; illustrated by William Pène du Bois
THE CIRCUS: A Book to Begin On by Mary Kay Phelan; illustrated by John Alcorn
COBWEB CASTLE by Jan Wahl; illustrated by Edward Gorey
COLL AND HIS WHITE PIG by Lloyd Alexander; illustrated by Evaline Ness
CONTRARY JENKINS by Rebecca Caudill and James Ayars; illustrated by Glen Rounds
EVAN'S CORNER by Elizabeth Starr Hill; illustrated by Nancy Grossman
JOHN JOHN TWILLIGER written and illustrated by William Wondriska
SAM, BANGS AND MOONSHINE written and illustrated by Evaline Ness
WHAT'S GOOD FOR A FOUR-YEAR-OLD? by William Cole; illustrated by Tomi Ungerer

Published simultaneously in Canada by Holt, Rinehart
and Winston of Canada, Limited.
Library of Congress Catalog Card Number: 65-21540

SBN: 03-080122-2

Printed in the United States of America
1 2 3 4 5 6 7 77 76 75 74 73 72 71

Coll and His White Pig

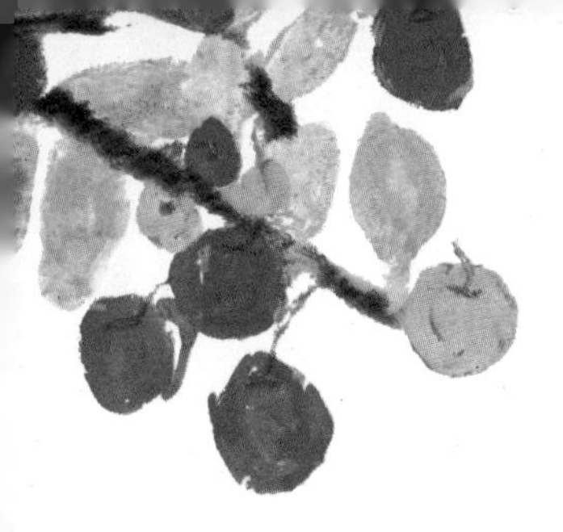

THIS IS THE BRAVE TALE of Coll and his white pig, and what befell them in the faraway Land of Prydain.

And this is the beginning of it.

Coll, in his younger days, had been a dauntless warrior. Now, grown a little stout around the middle, and much lacking in hair on the crown of his head, he had taken to farming.

"I have had my fill of wild adventuring, whatever," said Coll.

So he made a plow iron out of his sword and beanpoles from his old spears; and sparrows nested in his leather fighting cap. Not even Dallben, the most powerful enchanter in Prydain, had greater skill in plowing, planting, or harvesting than Coll. No man was as good-natured with a garden, as tender-hearted with a tree, or as agreeable with animals. He loved his vegetable plot, his apple orchard, and, above all, his white pig, Hen Wen.

One night, Coll had gone to bed worried over his turnips, which were coming up sickly that year; and he tossed and turned, wondering what to do about them. He was barely asleep when a thunder of hoofbeats aroused him. Next, he heard Hen Wen squealing at the top of her voice. Coll leaped up, pulled on his boots, flung a cloak around him, and was out the cottage door in a moment.

He glimpsed a band of horsemen galloping off into the forest. One rider had flung Hen Wen, shrieking and struggling, over his saddlebow. Shouting, Coll raced after them. For a time, he ran as fast as he could in the darkness, following the crashing of the steeds through the underbrush. But the riders outdistanced him and, at last, in the dawn mist, Coll dropped to the ground, out of breath, deeply distressed, having not the first notion of who had made off with his pig nor where they had taken her.

To restore his strength, Coll looked for roots and berries. Breakfast was a meal he always relished, but he found only a handful of hazel nuts. He had just finished munching them and was pondering what next to do, when he heard pitiful cries from a fallen tree nearby. An owlet was trapped in the tree trunk. Two owls fluttered desperately around it, but their efforts availed them nothing. Carefully, Coll freed the owlet and put it back in the nest, where the mother flew to join it.

The second owl perched on a limb above Coll's head. "My name is Ash-Wing," said the owl. "My wife and I thank you for your kindness."

"You are welcome to my help," said Coll, taken aback, "but I never thought owls could speak."

"Eggshells!" retorted Ash-Wing. "All creatures can speak. Until now, it is you who have not understood."

"How then?" said Coll, puzzled. "I have done nothing but munch a few hazel nuts, and meager fare they were."

"Surprising how little you humans know of such matters," replied the owl. "Those were Hazel Nuts of Wisdom. Only one tree in Prydain bears them. Luckily, you found it."

"Alas," said Coll, "I still have not wisdom enough to learn who stole my pig, or why."

"As to who," said Ash-Wing, "it was King Arawn of Annuvin, Lord of the Land of Death. As to why, it is because Hen Wen is no ordinary pig. She knows many deep secrets. Arawn has stolen her to find them out, and use them in his evil scheme to conquer all Prydain."

Coll turned pale and his blood ran cold. The Lord of the Land of Death was the enemy most dreaded throughout Prydain. "For the sake of Hen Wen, I would brave Arawn himself," said Coll. "But even if I could find my way, his guards would discover me before I set one foot within Annuvin." Coll put his head in his hands. "My pig is lost, and Prydain is doomed."

"Pinfeathers!" said Ash-Wing. "We owls know all the forest paths, and I will guide you to Annuvin. Under cover of darkness, you can slip past the guards. I will show you how, for I see better at midnight than other creatures see at noon. By the way, how many hazel nuts did you eat?"

When Coll replied that he did not know, Ash-Wing blinked at him. "Who but a human would eat them without counting! Let me tell you this: each nut is a day given you to understand the speech of birds and animals. When that power is gone, I can help no longer."

Hurriedly, Coll set out again with Ash-Wing on his shoulder. Though Coll's fear for his pig had grown greater, his heart also turned to his farm. "The worms will have their joy of my cabbages," said Coll to himself. "And blight on my beans. And scale on my apple trees. And my poor turnips—surely this is the end of them, whatever."

He had journeyed less than a day, following the owl's guidance, when a thrashing noise broke into his thoughts. A tall stag had caught his antlers in a thorn bush, and the more the creature struggled, the more he was entangled. Ash-Wing fluttered overhead while Coll, heedless of his torn garments and the deep scratches on his face and hands, ripped away the sharp thorns.

The stag leaped free, then bowed his head courteously to Coll. "My name is Oak-Horn," said the stag, "and I owe you my life. The Huntsmen of King Arawn ride abroad! Had they found me—my antlers tremble at the thought!"

"Tarry no longer," Ash-Wing cried to Coll. "Not only may the Huntsmen come upon us. The power of the hazel nuts may leave you before we reach Annuvin."

"Annuvin?" gasped Oak-Horn. "The very name makes my antlers wilt!"

When Coll told of his quest, the stag shuddered and rolled his eyes fearfully. "To be truthful," said Oak-Horn, "we stags are not—well, we are not the boldest folk in the forest. But we are the swiftest. If speed can help you, I will do my best."

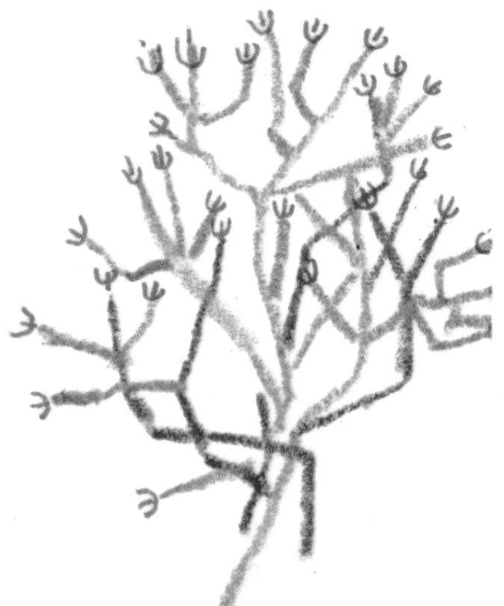

Oak-Horn bore Coll on his back and Ash-Wing perched atop the stag's antlers. As they quickly journeyed on, Coll yearned more and more for his comfortable chair by his warm fireside.

"And by this time," sighed Coll, "the beetles will be hard at work in my garden; that is, if they can find it under the weeds. As for my unhappy turnips—best not even think of them."

Suddenly, Oak-Horn reared up. A bird greater than the greatest eagle beat its wings and clawed savagely at a cleft rock. A tiny mole was cornered there, unable to flee or dig to safety. Coll sprang from Oak-Horn's back, snatched up a branch, and laid about him so furiously that the huge bird took flight.

"A gwythaint!" cried Oak-Horn, in such alarm that his antlers quivered. "One of King Arawn's messengers! It will carry news of us to the Land of Death. Ah, Coll, your quest is ruined. Ruined for a mere mole!"

"Mere mole indeed!" squeaked the little creature. "I am Star-Nose, Chief Mole of Prydain. In all our councils and clans, our fellowships and families, the name of Coll will be honored."

The mole scurried away. Ash-Wing urged all possible haste, and they set off once more. While the owl grumbled bitterly at the pridefulness of moles, and the stag shivered with fright at every step, Coll was silent and heavyhearted. He feared his gift of understanding might vanish at any moment. Even if it did not, the gwythaint would surely raise the alarm in Annuvin. "Yet I could do no less than help the unlucky mole," said Coll to himself, "and glad enough I was to do so. Nevertheless, honor to my name is no help to my pig and cold comfort to my turnips."

For some days they journeyed, Ash-Wing leading the way, Oak-Horn bearing Coll across rivers and along cruel mountain trails. At last, by night, they drew near the Dark Gate of Annuvin. Here, the owl spied out a hidden passage and the stag, despite quaking heart and quivering antlers, carried Coll down the twisting, treacherous path. Silent as shadows, they stole unseen into the depths of Arawn's realm.

Ash-Wing had flown ahead to find where Hen Wen had been taken. "Woeful news!" hooted the owl, returning. "She is prisoned in a deep pit, guarded by Huntsmen and fierce gwythaints. She is so terrified she cannot speak. Thus, Arawn has learned none of her secrets. But now he means to slay her."

"He shall slay me first!" cried Coll, leaping from the stag's back. "I will fight for my pig to the last!"

"Stay!" warned Ash-Wing. "First let me see what I may do."

Ash-Wing sped into the air. Catching sight of the owl, the gwythaints screamed with bloodlust and swooped to follow him.

Taking courage from Ash-Wing's example, Oak-Horn bounded forward. The Huntsmen shouted, drew their swords, and left the pit to pursue the stag.

Coll's way now lay clear. He raced ahead and flung himself into the unguarded pit, where Hen Wen squealed joyfully to see him. Desperately, Coll sought an escape for them. There was none. The pit was too deep; the walls were too sheer. Coll heard the clashing weapons of the returning Huntsmen, the beating wings of the gwythaints. All hope lost, Coll stood over his pig, vowing to sell his life dearly. Spears whistled down, arrows hissed, and Coll knew the end had come.

Suddenly, at his feet the pit opened. There stood Star-Nose and, behind him, moles in their dozens and hundreds and thousands.

"Quickly!" squeaked Star-Nose. "All our councils and clans, our fellowships and families have labored for you. Our tunnel will lead you to safety!"

Coll seized Hen Wen, thrust her into the mouth of the tunnel, and scrambled after. Behind him, Star-Nose and the others walled up the opening against the Huntsmen. At every turn, from every side, the moles cheered Coll and his white pig all along the way.

Far from Annuvin, the tunnel ended and they clambered above ground. Ash-Wing and Oak-Horn, having escaped unharmed, joined them again and began the journey back to Coll's farm. When at last they arrived at the edge of the woods, the owl and the stag halted.

"Farewell, Coll," said Ash-Wing. "If you ever need eyes to see in the darkness, call on me."

"Farewell, Coll," said Oak-Horn. "My heart is still in my mouth, but if you ever need a swift foot, call on me."

"And if you ever need work well done," piped up Star-Nose, who had been lying in a fold of Coll's cloak this while, "do not forget us."

"Farewell," said Coll. "I shall forget none of you."

He turned from the forest. The voices of his friends faded behind him and he knew, sadly, that his power to understand their speech had ended. Hen Wen, her stubby trotters flying, ran beside him, as he hastened to his farm.

Amazed, Coll stopped short. Not a weed did he see; nor, at a quick glance, any sign of worms in the cabbages, blight on the beans, or scale on the apple trees. Yet he was more alarmed than pleased, because smoke was curling out of the cottage chimney.

"Alas," cried Coll, dismayed, "I have found my pig and lost my farm."

He stepped past the door. A fire crackled merrily in the hearth, and in Coll's chair sat a gray-bearded stranger, so ancient that his hands seemed brittle as autumn leaves, his face lined like frost tracings on an ice-bound river. Though Coll was a bold man, he drew back a little fearfully before the flame of authority in the stranger's pale eyes.

"A good greeting to you, Coll," said the aged man, not troubling to get up. "If I had reached here sooner, I might have spared you a harsh journey. I sensed Hen Wen's danger and set out to warn you. I arrived a little late; but no matter. You have done well enough on your own. And I have whiled away the time tending your garden. You know me not," he added, seeing Coll's bewilderment, "but I know you, and the worth of your pig. I am Dallben."

Few in Prydain had looked face to face upon this mighty enchanter, and Coll bowed most humbly. For her part, Hen Wen sat on her haunches and grinned happily.

"No doing of mine," replied Coll, and he told what had befallen him along the way.

"Tut," said Dallben. "Look at the root of things, and see that what truly counts is not a strong arm but a kind heart; not a fist that smites, but a hand that helps."

The enchanter then pointed to a great leather-bound book on the table. "This is *The Book of Three,* and in it is set down all that will happen in the days to come. These things are hidden from you now, but I grant you the gift of knowing one of them. Which shall it be?"

Coll's bald head turned pink and he pulled nervously at his ear, for he was a modest man and unused to such favors.

"Now then," he answered, thinking hard, "I already know that spring will surely follow winter; and just as surely there will be sunlight and rain, good days and bad. And if I am to have any more such adventures—why, I would rather not know about them ahead of time. It is a great gift you offer me; but, thank you all the same, I have no need of it."

"Think well," said Dallben. "This chance will not be given to you again."

"Wait!" cried Coll. "Yes, there is one matter I would know above all. Tell me, then, tell me, for it has been on my mind these many days: how shall my turnips fare this year?"

Dallben smiled. "To answer that, I need not open *The Book of Three,*" he replied. "They will thrive."

It was true, even as Dallben had said. Coll's turnips had never been bigger or tastier. Dallben himself agreed to remain at the farm, which greatly pleased Coll—not only for the honor of it, but for the safety of Hen Wen. And all prospered.

"No doubt about it," said Coll to Hen Wen. "It is better to be raising things up than smiting things down. And quieter, into the bargain."

Such is the tale of Coll and the rescuing of Hen Wen, with the help of the owl, Ash-Wing, the stag, Oak-Horn, and the digging and delving of the moles.

And such is the end of it.

LLOYD ALEXANDER was born and brought up in Philadelphia, where he still lives. As a boy, one of his favorite pastimes was browsing in bookstores (it still is!) and one purchase he well remembers was a children's version of the King Arthur stories. That started his interest in tales of heroes and led him to the Mabinogion, the classic collection of Welsh legends—and finally the imaginary country of Prydain flowered from the diverse elements of his research and was set down in THE BOOK OF THREE (an ALA Notable Book), THE BLACK CAULDRON, and now COLL AND HIS WHITE PIG, his first picture book.

Mr. Alexander has published ten adult books and five juveniles. His particular interests are cats and music, and he has now taught himself some Welsh.

EVALINE NESS is the distinguished illustrator of ALL IN THE MORNING EARLY by Sorche Nic Leodhas, runner-up for the 1964 Caldecott Award and A POCKETFUL OF CRICKET by Rebecca Caudill, runner-up for the 1965 Caldecott Award.

A believer in variety, Miss Ness is always experimenting with new techniques, and has become an expert in many types of reproduction, including her own inventive methods of achieving a particular effect.

Miss Ness was born and grew up in Pontiac, Michigan. She studied for two years at the Art Institute of Chicago and for another two years at the Corcoran School of Art in Washington.